I0788177

The Internal

By

Bobbie Jo Kompardo

1-13946165201

Table of Contents

Chapter1:
It's a Gift & a Curse

It's a cool, breezy night. A young man appears he is our soon to be hero - Justin Young - 23 years old, dressed in ripped jeans, a gray muscle shirt under a black leather jacket with studs. His hair is a faded multi-colored mohawk, which he only styles when he is on the stage. He is walking out of the back door of a club. There's a sign on the club that reads 'live music.'

A large bouncer opens the door and he calls to him, "*Be careful out there, Justin don't drink yourself into trouble.*"

Justin, thinking to himself: "I know he is genuinely concerned".

Justin: *I'll be careful, have a good night, Tony*

Tony: *I still need to catch one of your shows not working the door*

Justin walks off into the night, a bottle of booze in hand. Walking past flyers for his show. He rips one down and looks at it. 'Freaks with Justin Young' and features a picture of him performing.

Justin, thinking to himself:

'I know Tony was genuine when he told me to be careful. The word is right, "care," only people that care about you tell you to be careful, but that's not how I knew...I could feel his feelings. That's what I do... I feel feelings. If only it was always easy, always a Tony simple brief reading of one's emotions but it's not. It's freaking torture, and that's why...'

He chugs the last of his bottle and throws it in a dumpster and wipes his mouth and pulls another small bottle of booze from his jacket pocket.

Justin finishes his narration, *'That's why I drink.'*

'When I was a kid, my parents would just say he's sensitive, but I knew the day I realized it was more.' Justin thinks of a memory.

3rd grade- playground- recess

9-year-old Justin is at the playground, he is on the slide with a little girl, and a group of young boys toss a football. The girl goes down the slide, and the class bully, Bobby, runs into her and knocks her down. Justin helps her up.

Justin: *'Hey, Watch where you're going.'* (he turns to the little girl) Roxanne, are you ok? The girl shakes her head yes.

Bobby: *'This area is for football, loser.'*

Justin: *'No, it's for the slide "loser."'*

That comment makes the other boys laugh, but Bobby feels disrespected.

Bobby: *'You're a wimp, Justin.'*

He pushes Justin down, and Justin absorbs the boys' anger. The kids crowd around and start chanting, "Fight, fight, fight!" Bobby goes to throw a punch, and he is big & strong. Justin is skinny & weak. Justin catches the punch in his hands, absorbs the power, and punches Bobby hard! A teacher breaks it up.

Teacher: *'You two principal's office now!'*

Later that day at Justin's home, he's being disciplined by his parents: *'We do not condone violence in this family, you're grounded.'*

Mother leaves the room, and father stays in.

Father: *'I just got one thing to say to you, young man. ..where did you learn to punch like that?'* His dad smiles, and Justin smiles back.

Now at night, Justin takes a walk.

Justin thinking to himself:

I am a hopeful person, but I struggle with depression, a simple walk down the street. I can feel joy, love and dark emotions. I can see how ugly some people can be on the inside and how much hurt some hold inside.

As Justin walks the streets, he encounters a homeless man on the curb, begging for change. Justin gives him a dollar. The man thanks Justin, *"God bless you"*.

Justin can feel the man's despair and loss, as well as his will to live barely there. His eyes tear up.

Justin continues his thoughts: *so much pain in the world, and I feel it all. And that leads me here on a bridge alone, drunk, wondering if I can ever lose my gift... my curse.*

Justin sits on the rail of a bridge, looking into the river

Justin: *'It's time to call it a night'*

He sips his bottle, and as he gets off the rail to leave, he slips and falls into the river.

Justin falls into the water and splashes like an anchor tossed into the sea. In the muddy river, all he sees is black. He tries to swim to the top, but he can not tell which way is up. Is he swimming to the surface or kicking further to the bottom? He tries to find the current, the water will find its way, but the water is still.

Justin, no longer able to hold his breath, sees the light shining through the muck. He reaches for the light, but his eyes close, and his body goes limp. Suddenly, there are bright lights, and he awakens. He's alive in the multiverse! He looks around at different colored lights, beauties, and oddities floating in space, and he hears a voice.

Voice: *'I've been waiting for you.'*

Justin: *'Me?'*

Voice: *'Yes, you, Justin welcome to the multiverse*

Justin rubs his eyes, he is confused.

Voice: *'Surely you didn't believe there's only one universe?'*

Justin: *'I...I guess not who... What are you? How do you know my name?'*

Voice: *'I know a lot more than your name, Justin Young, I know you.'*

The Voice emerges, showing itself. Tall and brawny, silver following hair, long beard like a wise wizard yet powerful like a Titan.

Voice: '*Allow me to introduce myself. I am the creator of the multiverse and everything in it. I am The Supreme Deity*'

Justin: '*Whoa.*'

Supreme Deity: '*I am Time and space, this multiverse is my creation. To Earth, I gave life. Those are my children many millennials ago, and I put all my focus and energy into forming your planet and your universe. I watched it from afar, and I learned how to nourish it. I tried different life forms.*'

(The Supreme Deity transforms the lights surrounding them to illustrate his words. The stars form to show dinosaurs, a meteor crashing down, causing the big bang. The stars then form to show the image of cavemen hunting, then snow..the big freeze.)

But life forms could not take care of the planet without me. They couldn't keep up with her existence. I have many planets in the multiverse, some with life forms, some with not, some simple, some complex. I can create, but it is up to the planet's inhibitors to keep the world going, and that's why I made the first humans, but before they were evolved enough to take care of their planet, I was needed somewhere else urgently

The Supreme Deity goes on to tell the story.

Supreme Deity: '*I did not want to leave the planet and have my creations suffer the same fate as others before, and then I was made an offer from Cacodemonic. He is a force from the dark dimension. I knew he was not one to deal with, but without someone to look over the humans that were just formed there's no way humankind would make it. Our deal was simple, Cacodemonic would be my lookout on Earth... immediately informing me of any convolutedness. We laid down our terms. The rules were set. My children would all be born with a soul. Something that would always bond them to me and to ensure Cacodemonic would not enslave them to him. My children would all have free will. Cacodemonic, in return, wanted to be the Earth's core, planting his ways all around them.*'

Justin: '*That's... Wow it makes sense so when I fell off the bridge I died and now I meet my creator. That's what the afterlife is?*'

Supreme Deity: '*Yes, and no, you did. In fact, die you are in fact, meeting your creator, but not everyone does. Afterlife, that's a complicated story for another time. You were here because you were born with a strong spirit. That is why you can sense others' feelings. You can peer into their souls, and there is a reason that you can do that and now I need you to fight off three veins of Cacodemonic as I tend to another planet.*'

Justin: (confused, scared) '*What? Me? Viens?!*'

Supreme Deity: '*Veins of Cacodemonic, he has set them up through the Earth's soil... pumping his evil blood into his servants. They will delineate Greed, Malice, and Slaughter. They are human but have all lost who they were when they accepted his blood gift. Those people are fueled by his promises and accelerated with hate. These three sycophants are out to multiply Cacodemonic's blood vessels and help him propagandize the human race. My creations, becoming his bond, servants in my absence, you can stop the three.. prevent them from creating more veins to feed evil into the unknowing mortals. You have been chosen to do this. You have only scratched the surface of your gifts, Justin.*'

Justin: '*I'm an empath, a musician...a drunk. How can I stop anyone, let alone three branches of a demonic force... you got the wrong dude.*'

Supreme Deity: '*You were born different, and for this reason, you nearly lost your way, letting feelings of sorrow drive you to over-drinking, but you did not despite falling from your predestined path. Despite feeling lost and hopeless, you stayed true to your goodness.*'

Justin: '*I'm not always good.*'

Supreme Deity: '*No, you are not. You are human, you are flawed, you are stronger than you think. Feeling the pain of others for all your years is enough to destroy nearly any mortal, but it did not destroy you. Do you, Justin Young, a man of a kind heart, stand before me and deny my request?*'

Justin: '*No I won't deny it, I want to help you, but I don't know how.*'

Supreme Deity: *'Again, I remind you, you have only scratched the surface of your powers. They should all be revealed, believe in me believe in good over evil believe in yourself.'*

Justin: *'I will ...I will try.'*

Supreme Deity: *'Justin Young, the Power is inside of you.'*

The Supreme Deity shoots Justin , back to Earth, charging him with energy. Justin looks at his hands, at the colorful lights on this journey back. The Supreme Deity's voice says one last thing as Justin lands on Earth.

"You are The Internal."

Chapter 2: Fallen To Earth

Justin lays on the riverbanks, and wipes dirt from his pants and stands up. His new, strong body was light, glowing white in his veins.

Justin: '*I feel strength from the supreme Deity, I feel (his head starts to spin, his eyes get heavy) I feel like I just traveled the Multiverse ... Drained.*'

Justin falls to the ground, his human body in need of much rest.

Not far away, a group of hoodlum teens is roaming the woods. There's one girl and two boys they're smoking weed from a soda can. The oldest of the teens starts to complain,"*This shit is lame. We should be snorting some perks, not hitting weed through a homemade bowl.*" The girl agrees: "*Yeah, well, thank the new guy, Nate here. His granny's in pain from her fall. At least he brought this pussy ass weed*". The younger-looking teen, Nate, says," *Is that the only reason you guys asked me to hang out to get my grandma's pain pills?*" The other male answers," *Oh yeah, duh.*" The girl continues to mock Nate," *and you didn't even come through man you should go back to Boy Scouts haha you're not down the party for real.*"

All of a sudden, the group sees a crack in the ground, and an orange light peers through. The leader of the teens is lured to the lights in the ground. He inserts his finger in the crack of the soil, and his eyes go white. Something/someone from below talks to him as the older teen touches the light. What they can't see is the trace back to where the light is emerging from. It leaks through the layers of the earth's crust. It resonates from a dark source. A voice whispers, "*Find him, destroy him. He is near.*"

The older boy, now in a trance, walks into the woods towards the river bay. The other two teens look at each other, confused. The girl calls out to him," *Chaz, where are you going? WTF?"*

Chaz looks at them with white eyes and says, *"Find him.. he is near.* "He takes the girl's hand, holds it tight, and pushes it into the orange light. Her eyes go white. She is now in a zombie-like trance. The younger teen, not that did not touch the orange light, looks around and hits the pop can bowl again, *"We're doing this shit now... OK."*

They follow the cracks in the ground with the orange light. It leads them to Justin, who is passed out from exhaustion. The two teens who are in a hypnotic state mutter, *"Find him... Destroy him"*. The girl picks up a rock and raises it above her head, ready to smash it into Justin as he is sleeping. The young teen, not affected, rushes in and grabs her arm to stop her.

The girl turns her head to Nate, and he sees her eyes all white and is frightened. Chaz holds a log above Justin's face, ready to smash him. Justin 's eyes open, he grabs the log and leaps to his feet. This is the start of the fight scene.

Justin beats Chaz to every punch and greatly outpowers him during the fight.

Nate stands back and watches as the girl hits Justin in the back with a broken boat paddle.

This causes Justin to hunch over, and Chaz takes the opportunity to kick Justin in the gut. Nate steps in, pushing Chaz away, *"Two-on-one isn't a fair fight."*

Chaz punches Nate in the face, and he wipes a small amount of blood from his nose. Angry, Nate yells at Chaz, "Oh, *you're gonna need your own pain pills now bitch!"*

Nate starts fighting Chaz. The girl attempts to attack Justin. Easily outpowering them all, Justin lifts Chaz by his shirt and swings him into the girl. They crash, and it knocks them out of the trance. Their eyes go back to normal, Chaz says to the girl. *" let's get the fuck out of here."*

They run off. Nate turns to Justin, "*I'm sorry, I didn't know they were going to attack a sleeping man. What are you doing sleeping on the river banks anyways, you a homeless?*

Justin: *I'm not homeless, kid. Are your friends on meth or something? What was up with her eyes?'*

Nate: '*They're not my friends. I just moved here and was trying to find people to hang with. And No, we didn't touch anything other than some weed. They started tweaking out when they touched something orange on the ground.'*

Justin, thinking to himself, realized that the evil from the earth's core must have gotten into the two hazed teenagers.

Justin: '*Go home kid... Don't hang with trouble like that.'*

Nate: '*Yeah, man, I won't.'*

Justin walks up to Nate, and takes a bag of weed out of his shirt pocket

Justin: '*Don't smoke weed, kid.'*

Nate: '*How did you know that was there? You know what... Never mind. Yeah, no more weed smoking.'*

 Justin: '*Your grandmother is waiting for you kid to get home.'*

Nate, stunned, turns around and runs home. Justin grabs a one-hitter from his jacket and smokes his newly found weed.

Chapter 3:
Creed

It's morning, Justin is in his apartment, looking in the mirror and admiring his new hot bod. He starts talking to himself.

Justin: '*This is crazy. I'm going to stop Cacodemonic from taking over Earth while The Supreme Deity is away. How? Where do I even start?*'

He sits at a small table where his breakfast bowl of cereal is awaiting. A sharp breeze blows open a nearby window.

Voice: '*You start by following the cracks.*'

Justin: 'Ok, now I'm hearing voices.'

The wind forms a face, and a spirit appears. It is cloud-like and slightly transparent, with the face of a woman. Making herself visible to Justin.

Voice: '*More than a voice Internal, I'm Nadia, your spirit guide, the supreme deity, sent me to educate you for your quest.*'

Justin: '*Cool, my own personal spiritual guide. Nice to meet you Nadia, so I follow the cracks from last night that glow orange?*'

Nadia: '*Exactly, and as for how that will be using your intuition, empathy and gifts, you have yet to discover. Much to learn internally and to develop. Trust in synchronicity.*'

Justin: '*Synchronicity?*'

Nadia: '*The signs ...the meaningful coincidences.*'

Just then, the TV turns on by itself. The local news is on, and a reporter on the news says the following:

"*Governor and presidential candidate Harold Creed is making a visit in the city to speak about our growing homeless population, although he has been under much scrutiny for spreading hate onto the vagrant community."*

The news now shows Harold Creed, talking into the camera

Creed: *'Listen, I don't hate the homeless. Some of them could be wonderful people. The fact of the matter is we need to take our streets back for normal tax paying citizens to enjoy because that's the people that matter.'*

Justin: *'He means the people registered to vote. Those are his people that "matter."'*

As Justin watches the news pan out, he notices something in the building behind Creed. There's a thin crack in the pavement. No one else noticed but Justin does, and he sees the crack, beaming orange.

Justin: *'Follow the cracks looks like the cracks lead to Harold Creed.'*

Nadia: *'This is quite a meaningful coincidence. We've just located one of the three veins of Cacodemonic, Harold Creed, born with a demonic attachment. Creed is the vein of greed, and he steers minds into fear and anger. This is the fuel that has been cast by other men of power before. There has not been a mortal with that kind of demonic attachment with so much potential to get a mass following since ...(she pauses).'*

Justin: *'Since when Nadia?'*

Nadia: *'April 20, 1889 the birth of Adolphus Hitler.'*

Justin: *'I got to stop him!'*

Justin raises his fist

In the boiler room in Harold Creed's building, an orange light is glowing from a crack in the cement floor. Creed kneels down and listens to a voice coming from the light.

Voice: Harold Creed, you are well on your way to fulfilling your chosen destiny. Do not forget your part of this deal. Cacodemonic is giving you everything you want: power, glory, and riches. You must hold up your end and deliver thousands of souls to him.

Creed: I will not disappoint my master. I have my plan in action, and thousands of homeless will be forced to give up their souls.

***Voice**: Go, use your gifts of persuasion, your liegemen await upstairs.*

Creed leaves, and upstairs in his office, he meets with 2 of his powerful allies,Ron and Johnathan. Both men play important roles in Creed's plan. Creed settles into his chair, ready to start the meeting. On walks, Justin disguised as a delivery man bringing in boxes of food.

Ron: *'This is a private meeting.'*

Justin: *'Um.. delivery.'*

Ron: *'Lay it over there.'*

Justin takes his time laying out the food, hoping to overhear the meeting

Creed: *'What are you doing making the table get out of here? Important men have business to discuss.*

We don't need our precious time waiting on some lower-class delivery boy to do his simple job.' Justin turns to leave and holds his hand out to Ron

Justin thinks to himself *' if I can make skin contact, I should be able to connect with his aurora for brief audio."*

Ron: *'You wanna tip, huh? Here's a tip: watch out where the Huskies go, and don't you eat the yellow Snow.'*

The men laugh. Justin shakes the man's hand and says, *"Good one, sir. I'll remember that."*

Justin leaves his sweaty hand, which glows purple. His transfer of energy worked. Justin goes outside the building and sits in the alley where Nadia is. Justin rubbed his hand. It tapped into the man's aurora enough for Justin to be able to hear what was being said inside.

The men in the meeting go on to reveal their plans.

Creed: *'As you see, followers, I am confident in my road to the White House and once I'm there, I will start operation government required housing. All homeless will be forced into our company's housing community, which will be paid for by taxpayers. When our* project starts, we will do the impossible: make a profit off the homeless. I'll be taking their freedom, liberties, and more (their souls). *And let's not forget our housing will be able to get rid of these free, loading rats off the city streets into our designated area, where they will work to keep roofs over their heads.'*

Ron: '*Modern day slavery. I love it!'*

Creed: '*What's not to love? This is only the beginning; men like us will be on top again, back to the days of royals & peasants. And men, we will be the royalty.'*

Outside, Justin and Nadia are listening.

Nadia: '*I believe it's time to use your new powers. This needs to stop before greed and intolerance influence others.'*

Justin: '*I'll get the evidence we need to expose their scam.'*

Justin runs off, waiting for the men to exit the building

Nadia: '*It's not that easy, internal.'*

The men leave and lock the door, Justin ponders how to get in

Nadia: '*You know the supreme deity created the sun and use its power.'*

Justin raises his hand to the sky. Heat from the sun enters his hand. Justin tells Nadia to wait outside. He places his hands on the metal door, and the lock melts. Once inside, Justin inserts a drive into the computer and starts going through papers on a desk.

Creed enters the office and sees Justin

Creed: '*What the hell?'*

The other two men enter the room, and a brawl begins.

Creed's eyes go white.

Creed: '*You're no delivery boy..you are the one that fell to the Earth.'*

Justin: '*Am I still talking to Creed, or an even bigger asshole?'*

Creed: '*You speak to the vein that pumps straight to the Lord of the core, he who will spread all over this Earth, and make it his own to conquer.'*

The other two men charge. Johnathan holds Justin 's arms behind his back while Ron punches him in the stomach, Justin can see the rage in Ron's eyes and feels his rage where it developed. He can see a memory of Ron as a child, with his father beating him up.

Justin: *'You're not your father.'*

Ron stops it and looks confused

Ron: 'How do you know about my daddy?'

Just then, Justin flips the other men over his head, releasing his arms. Justin blocks and holds Ron's fist and grits his teeth.

Justin: 'I *know a lot more than don't eat the yellow Snow.'*

Justin slams the man across the room. Both men are down. Creed gets up and smacks Justin with an office chair. Justin falls, and very quickly gets back up.

Creed: *'You won't get me down, fallen one, you think you are chosen, but you are a mere mortal.'*

Creed smacks Justin across the room, breaking a window. Justin struggles to get up, but this time, Nadia blows in and awakens Justin.

Nadia: *'It's time to unleash your gifts.'*

Justin sources power into his hands feeding off Creed's anger to absorb and use it against him. Creed raises a fist, but before it can get close enough to connect, Justin slides and kicks out Creed's knee.

Creed: *'You will not prevail. These humans are blank, and slates weak, suggestive that this allows us in. This is how we conquer.'*

A crack opens up wide in the floor and pulls Creed into the abyss.

The next morning in Justin's apartment, he is eating cereal. Suddenly the TV clicks on.

Reporter: *'Two men have been obtained after last night's disturbance at Harold Creed's headquarters although it is believed that creed himself has invaded the law. Evidence turned into channel 12 news shows a large list of felonies & fraud, executed by Creed and his accomplices.'*

Nadia appears in the kitchen

Nadia: *'Job well done Internal.'*

Justin: *'Internal, I still gotta get used to being called that.'*

Chapter 4:
Malix

It's morning, the sun is shining through the window, and two young lovers are lying in bed. The man caresses the woman's face. The man's name is Will, the woman's name is..Malix

Will: *Good morning gorgeous* (looking into her bright green eyes).

Malix; (smiling) *Good morning, handsome. You better get ready for work.*

Will kisses her lips

Will: I *could be a little late.*

(He pulls the blankets up over them. Malix giggles)

Later that afternoon Malix is having lunch with her girlfriend, Emily.

Emily: *Listen, I know you're happy, but let's be realistic here. He's been married three times. Major red flags girl.*

Malix: *Yes, but that was years ago. The first one chose her career over keeping the marriage, the second one cheated on him, and the third one used him for his money.*

Emily: *All three was the ex-wife's fault?*

Malix: *Yes.*

Emily: *Listen to yourself... He's always the victim. How do you think it will be any different with you?*

Malix: *Because I'm different, and he has evolved emotionally.*

Emily: *I hope you're right I do want you to be happy. I'm just looking out for you, Malix.*

Malix: I *appreciate it, Emily, but your concern is unnecessary.*

Later that night, the two lovers, Will & Malix, lay in bed watching TV. Malix tells him about her conversation with her friend Emily.

Will: *Your friend is not looking out for you, Malix. She's just jealous that you're happy, and she's not.*

Malix: *No, Emily is not like that, Will. Let's just go out for dinner. It's been nearly a year, and you still haven't met any of my friends, not that I see them much anymore. All we do is sit in the bed talking and watching TV.*

Will: *We do a lot more than just watch TV in this bed.*

He kisses her and lights go out.

The following afternoon, Malix is at her job in a restaurant, busing tables and two waitresses are talking to each other and looking at her. Malix thinks to herself, 'great, I have to work with these two! Bonnie and Donna, I swear they are the mean girls of the workplace.'

The waitresses eye up Malix while talking to each other about her.

Bonni: *You almost feel sorry for her.*

Donna: *But not really* (they laugh).

Malix thinking to herself: *'OK, am I being paranoid or are they talking about me? Yeah I'm over thinking why would they be talking about me? There's plenty of "her"s they could be talking about that's silly. the world doesn't revolve around me.'*

Malix walks towards the woman with a tub full of dirty dishes. As she passes, the waitress continues to talk to each other.

Bonni: Well, *you know what they say... once a cheater, always a cheater.*

After work, Will picks up Malix.

Will: *How was work, gorgeous?*

Malix*: Exhausting*

Will: *I'm sorry babe, let's get you home. I'll get a hot bath ready and you can relax with a glass of wine.*

Maix: *sounds awesome. I do need to stop at the store on the way.*

(she kisses him on the cheek)

Will: *Anything you want, babe!*

Malix is in the store, buying a bottle of wine., A barbarous woman, amazing in stature, angrily storms up to her, pushing her buggy in front of Malix.

Woman: *So you're the new one?*

Malix: *Excuse me?*

Woman: *Will's new girl, the other girl... I mean, you don't actually believe you're the only woman in his life*

Malix: *What?*

Woman: (yelling) *Maybe you should find out where he goes while you're at work girl.* Malix leaves the store and enters the car, visibly upset. Will is in the car waiting.

Malix: *You won't believe what just happened to me in there some crazy large woman came up to me mad and ...*

(Her sentence is cut off by a soda can being thrown at the back window of the car; it's the woman from the store.)

Woman: *I see Will get 'em while they're young and cute.'*

The woman continues to carry on a scene. Will and MaliX speed off in the car.

Malix: *Who is that woman? What the hell is going on?*

Will: *Nothing.*

Maix: *Well "nothing" just threw something at our car!*

Will:'*She's just some deranged crackhead or something.*

Malix: *She knew your name.*

Will stops talking. He pulls up to the house and opens Malixs's car door

Malix: *Tell me the truth, Will, now!*

Will: *She's a woman I work with and she was obsessed with me. I didn't like her like that, she went crazy.*

Malix: *You're just now telling me this?*

Will: I *didn't want to upset you. She's nothing she's not worth mentioning.*

Malix: *When did all of this happen?*

Will: *Over a year ago.*

Malix: *More than a year ago, and she's still obsessed with you?*

Will: *Yes, she must've seen your picture on my desk.*

Malix: *I'm reporting this.*

She picks up the phone, and Will hangs it up.

Will: *there's no need to get the cops involved*

Malix*: she just confronted me in the store and damaged the car. She's a psycho. We should report it in case she does it again.*

Will: *Nothing will happen again, just ignore her, and she'll go away.*

Will hands Malix a glass of wine

Will: *Now let's get you that hot bath and a foot rub you had a long day.*

(Kisses her)

The next day, Will drives Malix to work

Will: *Have a great day, gorgeous!*

Malix: *You too!*

They kiss. Malix enters her work and sees the two bitchy waitresses talking to someone. The person turns around, and it's the woman from the store. She's there picking up takeout.

Malix thinking to yourself, "Oh, *hell, no, I can't afford to cause a scene and lose my job. Maybe it's just a coincidence."*

The woman leaves, turning her head and glaring at Malix on her way out of the restaurant.

Bonnie: '*Hi Malix.'*

Malix thinking to herself: '*Weird they are talking to me, that's unusual.'*

Donna: *Your hair looks super cute today.*

Malix again thinking to herself '*being nice that's very unusual.*'

Bonnie: *So who dropped you off for work, your boyfriend?*

Malix: *Yeah, he drops me off every day, you just noticed?*

Donna: *Well, we're not always paying attention. We get busy serving tables. You know it takes more focus than just busing the tables.*

The two waitresses laugh.

Bonnie: I *didn't even know you had a boyfriend Malix.*

Donna*: You should come out with us for a drink after work.*

Malix: (surprised, but happy) Um *sure I'll just let my boyfriend know.*

The two waitresses take off and start waiting tables. Malix starts to text Will.

Text on the phone call reads:

M: Hey, pick me up at eight instead of seven going to have a drink with the girls from work.

W: OK, have fun. Love u!

M: Love u too!

Later that evening after work, Malix sits with the two waitresses, having a drink.

Malix: So *today, when I came in, there was a woman getting takeout.*

Bonnie: *Oh, what one? We had a lot of takeout orders today.*

Malix: *The one you were both ringing up when I started my shift.*

The two waitresses in sync: *oooh.*

Donna*: Her name is Jane.*

Malix: *You know her. Don't tell me you are friends with her.*

Donna: *No, she used to work there. She got fired for stealing.*

Malix: *What? Wow.*

Bonnie: She's *always causing drama. I'm surprised she still shows her face there.*

Donna: *Why are you asking about Jan, Malix. Do you know her?*

Maix: *Well...*

They continue the conversation. Malix tells them about her encounter with Jan the night before

Malix thinking to herself: '*It feels good to get it off my chest other than the rare occasion I meet my old friend for lunch. I don't talk to anyone other than Will anymore. This is nice work, friends.*'

Bonnie: '*o tell us how you and your boyfriend met.*

Donna: *And when.*

Malix thinking to herself: '*They actually want to know about my relationship, my life... cool.*'

Malix: Last *spring, I met Will, and we became inseparable. I was saving money and about to sign up for a few courses at a community college, and Will asked me to move in with him.*

Bonnie: So *what happened to the community college plan?*

Malix: I *decided to wait another year.*

Donna: *At least you have the money saved up for it.*

Malix: *Well, not really. I spent it on a car.*

Bonnie: *You don't even drive, and you bought a car?*

Malix: *I don't drive, but Will does, and he takes me anywhere I need to go.*

Donna: *So you bought Will a car.*

Malix: No, I *bought us a car. Besides, I do live in his house. The least I can do is buy us a car.*

The three continue the talk. Malix becomes an open book, and then she checks her phone. It's 7:55 PM.

Malix: I *gotta go. My boyfriend is picking me up.*

Donna gets out her phone, starts the text, and giggles to herself

Bonnie: *OK, Malix, see you at work.*

Malix: *Not tomorrow. I'm off.*

Donna puts down her phone.

Donna: *You got plans to spend your day off with Will?*

Malix: *No, unfortunately, he will be at work. I'll spend the day alone reading. I just started a new book.'The life of a vampire.'*

Bonnie: *'Well, enjoy your day off.'*

Malix: *Thanks.*

Maix goes outside, waiting for a ride 8:10 PM still no Will 8:25 PM she sends her third text to Will the text reads, "Hello?".Will pulls up.

Will: *I'm so sorry gorgeous, I fell asleep.*

Malix gets in the car.

Next day, Malix's day off, she goes to grab the book. She's been reading. As she pulls it out, a card falls from inside the book. The card has a heart on it. She opens it up, and it reads:

"To Will, just a note to say I love you XOXO Jan."

Malix's eyes open wide up.

Malix: *WTF!*

Meanwhile at the restaurant ,the waitresses are talking and giggling with Jan.

Bonnie: *So we got her out of the house last night. Did you enjoy yourselves?*

Donna: *She didn't suspect a thing, even when he showed up late .. naïve bitch.*

Jan: *Well, I left a little something behind.*

They laugh, and the manager walks over and starts talking to Jan.

Manager: *What are you doing here? You got fired, so you don't need to be coming in here.*

Jan: *I just came to bring my friend some cookies.*

Jan points to the cookies, and the manager points to the door.

Jan:*'Bye girls.*

And she leaves.

Back at the house. Will walks in from work, and Malix is waiting for him, holding the note.

Malix: *You lying piece of shit! "we work together"?*

Will : *What are you talking about?*

Malix: *I found her love card for you… I can't believe you messed with that pig and lied straight to my face.*

Will : I *didn't lie about anything.*

Malix: *Oh yeah, then how do you explain this?*

She shoves the card into his chest

Will: *She left it on my desk.*

Malix:*'Then what is it doing here? Why won't you take it up if she's so obsessed & psycho?*

Will : I *kept it for evidence to give to HR. Here, throw it away. You are the only woman I want. I love you, but you need to fix your trust issues. I know. I understand why you have them, but not all men are liars and cheaters.*

Malix, wiping away tears, hugs will.

Malix: I'm sorry.

Will: *It's OK. Hey, I bought you something it's on the porch.*

He takes her out to the porch and shows her a potted bush

Will: *It's a rose bush I mean I was going to get your roses and I thought why not just get the whole bush*!

Malix: *Thank you, I love it!*

The next day, Malix is planting the rosebush, she sees something bright orange very deep in the ground. She looks at it curiously. She pricks her finger on a thorn, and a tiny drop of blood falls into the orange shining from the ground. She finishes planting the bush and hears a voice coming from the rose.

Voice: Malix...walking through life with blinders on. Poor soul.

Malix, confused, not sure if she is hearing voices, leans down to the rose bush, it glows brighter and brighter.

Voice: You're not crazy, Malix, you're weak.

Malix: Ok...this is not real. I need to get out of this heat and get ready for work.

Voice: THIS is real! When you're ready to go from victim to victor, I will be here. With a deal you can't refuse.

Malix rubs her eyes and squints, shakes her head and enters the house and gets ready for work. When she arrives at the restaurant. Her parents are both at a table waiting for her.

Malix: *Mom, Dad, what are you doing here...early dinner?*

Mom: *Malix, we need to talk.*

Malix*: I start work in 10 minutes.*

Dad: I *know we'll be quick.*

Malix sits down at the booth with both of her parents

Dad*: We got an anonymous letter in the mail yesterday... About you.*

Malix: *Me? OK.*

Mom*: It said Will is a dangerous man and that he's been married three times and you used your school money to buy him a car.*

Malix: *What, who sent this letter? This is gossip. You're at my job, interrogating me about my money and my boyfriend.*

Dad: *Sweetie, calm down, we're just here because we're concerned.*

Malix*: Who sent the letter?!*

Dad: I *told you it was anonymous with the out-of-state postmark.*

Mom*: Probably a friend that was worried about you. Maybe it was Emily.*

Malix*: Then Emily needs to mind her own business. I need to start my shift.*

Malix walks away, very upset and angry. Later that day, the waitresses talk to Malix.

Bonnie*: Who do you think sent your parents that letter?*

Malix: I *don't know, just a lot of strange things have been happening ever since I had that run in with that crazy Jan woman who's obsessed with Will.*

Donna: *So you think she did it?*

Bonnie: *But she doesn't know about the car in the class, she's just a random crazy, right.*

Malix: *Yeah, I guess she wouldn't know that personal stuff.*

Donna: I think your folks are right it was probably your friend Emily.

Malix: Oh, by the way, I tried to call you last night and it went straight to voicemail.

 Bonnie: *I don't answer unknown numbers, and I don't have your number, so it was unknown.*

Malix: *Oh, I thought you would call me back, I left a voicemail.*

Bonnie: *I don't check voicemails either.*

Later that evening, Will and Malix are laying in the dark bedroom with the TV on. Malix tells Will about the letter.

Will: *I told you, Emily is jealous of us. She's trying to break us up, so you can just spend more time with her.*

Malix: *You're right.*

Will: *You should text her right now and tell her it's not going to work.*

Will hands Malix her phone

Will: *Do it you'll feel better.*

Malix's text to Emily reads:

M: ' can't believe you did that!

E: What I do a lot of unbelievable things lol.

M: The letter.

E: What letter?

M: Don't be coy, nice try but your attempt to come between me and Will won't work. E: WTF... Are you talking about?

Emily calls her phone. Will sees it and hits the decline button.

Will: *Don't let her talk her way out of this. She'll just try to blame someone else.*

Malix: *I know I'm pissed, but I should at least give her a chance to explain.*

Will: *No, block her; keep negative people out of your life, Malix.*

Malix looks at the phone. Emily is calling again, Will takes the phone out of her hand and hits a block. Malix looks sad and goes to sleep.

The following morning, Malix is outside trimming the rosebush, thinking to herself:

'Gardening will ease my stress. When did my life get so stressful? I know the day I went to the store and was minding my own business, I was verbally attacked by a large crazy woman.'

Malix sees the bright orange appear in the soil again, and she leans in to take a closer look. She puts her finger inside. She hears the voice again coming from the orange light.

Voice: *Malix, open your eyes. They are all lying to you. Give me more blood and see the truth.*

Malix looks at her hand, grabs pruning scissors, and makes a decent-sized cut along the palm of her hand. She places her hand over the orange light and squeezes his blood into it. As the blood hits the orange the light turns red, then back to orange.

Voice: *They all think you're a fool.. show them... show them all.*

The voice shows her images, thoughts, flashes of memories, the waitresses, talking to Jan waitress, one saying, Jan brought us cookies. The card that was lying in her book. The waitress is asking her out, Malix says she would be reading the book on her day off, the truth, the whole, wicked truth, Malix, with her hand, seeping blood into the soil just had a painful realization. She starts to cry, puts her hands to her face, and then sees her own blood now covering her hands and face. She goes from sadness and despair to anger. The soil speaks again.

Voice: *pretend to be the fool still and get even on them! I will show you how to guarantee you success in your retribution and how* *to not take the blame for it. In return, Cacodemonic will call out to you and you will find more people like the ones that deceive you. Together you will get measure for measure.*

Malix: *How do I do that?*

Voice: *Cacodemonic will lead you to these degenerates, you will capture their souls for him. or you can just keep letting everyone in your life walk all over you...doormat!*

Just then, Will pulls into the driveway.

Voice: There he is...coming back from being with Jan. A mouthful of lies ready to serve up to you. Are you going to take that Malix, or are you going to take the deal and get revenge!?

Malix is angry and hurt peers at Will exiting the car. She looks down at the rose bush.

Malix: DEAL

Voice: Good Choice.

Will walks up to Malix.

Will*: 'Hey gorgeous.'*

Malix wipes her face. Will sees the blood

Will: *Oh my God, are you OK?*

Malix: *Yeah, I'm fine, just a cut.*

Will: *Let's get you cleaned up.*

Malix looks Will in the eyes, and her eyes are different now, a deeper Shade of Green.

Malix: *Actually, dear, I think I'll get a shower care to join me?*

Malix gives him a sexy smirk, and Will follows her into the house excitedly.

Will: *Oh yes, I'll join.*

Inside the steamy bathroom, hands press upon the glass of the shower door.

We hear Will through the shower saying, "Oh my."

Malix exiting the shower.

Malix: *I'm going to dry off, take your time and clean up.*

Will: *Wow yes that was not like before. Yeah, I'll clean up.*

Malix grabs a towel. She reaches into Will's pants that are on the floor, and she grabs his cell phone to scroll down and find deleted messages text between Will & "Jimmy" with □emoji

Malix thinking to herself *'I never heard of a friend named Jimmy, a codename obviously.'* The text reads:

Jimmy: *can't wait to see you again Kissy face emoji*

Will: *I'll let you know when.. things need to calm down around here first.*

Jimmy: *Why don't you just dump her and get it over with already?*

Will: *It's complicated, she's too sensitive. I will do it… Soon, love you.*

Jimmy: *'Love you, Willie bear,' Kissy face emoji.*

Malix holding the phone thinking to herself: 'OK, Jimmy… Maybe it's time for another hook up,' She texts back as Will.

Text.

Will: *8 PM tonight don't text back. See you at 8 PM at my place.*

Malix hits send and delete and puts the phone back in his pants pocket. Malix yells into the shower: *"I'm taking a walk."*

Malix walks along the city street. She stops in several stores, a bakery, a salon, a pharmacy, and a boutique with sexy outfits in their window.

Malix's phone rings. She answers, it's Bonnie

Malix: I *thought you didn't have my phone number.*

Bonnie: *Hey, what are you doing tonight? And yeah, I got your number from work. Just didn't set you as a contact yet.*

Malix: *I'm getting into something.*

Bonnie: *Come to the club with us tonight, say eight sharp.*

Malix thought to herself, eight sharp, haha, they took the bait.

Malix: *Actually, how about seven? I'll see you then.*

When Malix returns home, Will is in bed, eating popcorn and watching TV.

Malix: *Honey, I'm home.*

Will looks at her shadowy figure in the hallway, as she steps into the light.

Will: *You look... Damn!*

Malix has a whole new look. Her once brown hair is now black with green highlights, she's wearing makeup, and her modest clothes have been replaced. She's wearing a tight, low-cut black top with skirt, thigh, high stockings, and heels.

Will: *What did you do? I mean, I love it, it's just this is what you did on your walk.*

 Malix: *This and some shopping.*

She lays down her bags

Malix: *I just felt the need for a change.*

She removes items from the bakery bag and starts whipping frosting in a bowl

Will: *Well, I like it.*

(He leans in to give her a kiss)

As Malix is whipping the ingredients in the bowl, she grabs her cell and holds it behind her back.

Malix: *You know, Will, not to bring up a sore subject, but I did want to talk about something or should I say someone.*

Will: *Oh really again? I told you I kept that card to give to HR.*

Malix: No, not that well yes that you're getting pissy with me just for talking about her yet when you talk about her there's no anger.

Malix hits dial on her phone that she has behind her back

Will: *I am angry!*

Malix: *She damages the car. She should pay for what she did.*

Malix's phone calls Bonnie and gets voicemail as she wanted. Now it is recording everything Will is saying.

Will: Yes, I am angry Jan, she should pay for what she did. That woman is a waste of human life...she's sickens me!

Malix hangs up her phone, leaving the voicemail of Will"s "hatred" for Jan.

Malix: *That's all I wanted (she grabs Will's head and kisses his forehead.) I just wanted to know if it made you just as mad as it made me and that you're in my corner.*

Will: *Always in your corner babe.*

Will stick his finger in the frosting

Will: *Baking?!*

He licks his finger and Malix pulls the bowl away from him.

Malix: *Yes, and I'll make you your very own frosted cookie. Oh, and I'm going out tonight with the girls from work.*

Will: *Oh, no, you're not not dressed like that.*

Malix: *Oh, yes, I am.*

Will: *Then I'm coming with you.*

Malix: *' will only be an hour. I don't want to stay out long, and you will stay here. The season premiere of your show starts at eight.*

Will: *Oh yeah, I can't wait. You had better be back in time for me to have round two with the new you.*

He hugs her and squeezes her butt. Malix kisses him long and deep, looking at him as if it's the last time she'll ever see him.

Will returns to the bed, watching TV in the dark. Malix walks in with a bakery box & a plate, and she hands Will the plate, which has a large decorated cookie on it

Malix: *Just as I said, your own special cookie.*

Will grabs the cookie and starts eating it like a pig

Malix: *I'll be back soon.*

Will: *OK love you.*

Malix leaves with the bakery box, she arrives at the club; the waitresses Bonnie & Donna are at the table and give her a fake greeting.

Malix: *I brought you cookies! I heard that's what your friends do lol.*

Bonnie*: Hell, yeah.*

Donna: *Oh, I better not.*

Malix: *Can't drink on an empty stomach.*

Donna: *Well, maybe but I did have pizza today, so no.*

Malix pushes the cookie box in front of Donna

Malix: *Just eat a goddamn cookie.*

Donna picks up the cookie and starts to eat. Malix sits down and checks the time on her phone, 7:05 PM.

Malix: *How about we get some shots to wash those down.*

Donna: *Yeah.*

Malix:*I'll grab them just gotta hit the lady's room first.*

Inside the lady's room at the club Malix sprinkles itching powder on the toilet paper and rolls it back with a smirk on her face.

While at Will's house, he is watching TV, when his eyes begin to close, he goes limp, and his popcorn spills.

Back at the club, lady's restroom waitresses are in the stalls, and Malix is out by the sink.

Bonnie: *Oh, God.*

Donna: *I need more toilet paper!*

Bonnie: *Why is it itching?*

Malix hands over a roll above the stall and smiles.

Malix thinking to herself: *'They're going to have a shitty night., thanks to my laced cookies. Laxatives are working and should mix nicely with the sleeping pills. Now, I got to sneak out to see if the omega comatose pills worked in Will's special cookie.'*

Malix takes the keys from the waitresses purse, gets in her car, and drives off next. Malix enters her house and sees Will is passed out in bed

Malix: *Hello gorgeous.*

Malix puts on rubber gloves and checks the time. It's 8:01 PM. Jan is calling for Will from the next room.

Jan: *Will I'm here, my friends are keeping the stupid Cunt busy so we can get busy.*

Jan enters the room, shocked to see Malix standing there holding a gun.

Malix: *Surprise Jan… "Stupid Cunt" has a gun.*

Jane: *You killed Will!*

She runs over to Will. Malix holds a gun to Jan's head

Malix: *Bite him.*

Jan: *What*

Malix: *I said, bite him right there on the arm.*

Jan*: It's not what you think, Malix. We can be friends, best friends, real sisterhood, isn't that what you want?*

Malix: I *said bite.*

Jane bites Will's arms.

Malix: *Now, scratch*

Jan lightly scratches Will's forearm.

Malix:'Now, *his upper arm and neck and hard I want to see it bleed.*

Jan complies

Jan: *He said you were trash, and he was leaving you.*

Malix: He *is leaving me… and you, you fat trouble-making whore you are leaving this world.*

Malix places the gun in Will's hand bang. Malix shoots Jan in the head, one shot dead. The gun smokes. Malix removes her gloves and gets back in the car

Back at the club, the waitresses are still in the stalls, sleepy on the toilet. Malix places the keys back in the waitress's purse

Malix: *Hey, come on, don't fall asleep on the shitter.*

She knocks on the stall doors and helps them to stumble out of the restroom. Malix puts her arms around them. Come on, girls, we are here to party. She takes them over to the table and brings them over drinks.

Malix: *OK, vodka and Red Bull, drink up*

Bonnie & Donna are itching.

Donna: *Oh, I'm so itchy.*

Bonnie: *'I'm scratching raw skin at this point.'*

Malix: *Can't trust public restrooms.*

(Smiles)

The girls take a drink.

Malix: *Bonnie, can I borrow your phone? My battery's almost dead.*

Bonnie slides over her phone. Malix picks up the phone

Malix: *You have a voicemail?*

She hits play on the voicemail. It's Will's voice.

Voicemail, please as follows:

"I am angry, Jane, she should pay for what she did. That woman is a waste of human life… She sickens me."

The girl's eyes get wide.

Donna: *That sobered me up WTF?*

Malix: *Oh, I must've butt dialed you.*

Bonnie: *Was that Will… Flipping out?*

Malix: *Yeah, shortly before I left, he was on some raging bender talking about that Jan lady.*

Donna: *He sounds crazy, like for real.*

Shortly later, the women leave the club. While driving up to Malix's house, they see police cars and yellow tape

Bonnie: *OMG!*

Malix jumps out of the car.

Malix: *That's my house, that's my house!*

Police: *Miss, please don't pass the tape try to calm down.*

EMT brings out Jan's covered deceased body. Police bring Will out, cuffed, kicking and screaming

Will: I *don't know what you're talking about. I was watching a TV show, that's all.*

The police start interviewing waitresses

Bonnie: *Yes, he is crazy. He left his deranged voicemail tonight.*

Cop: *And where were you at 8 PM?*

(asking Malix)

Donna: *At the club with me and Bonnie.*

Cop: *Just the club since 8 PM?*

Malix*: Yes, we met there at 7 PM*

Malix acting, sad wipes, her face with her hand with the scar from the cut she had earlier from the rose bush.

Later in the police interrogation room the female DA informs Will it's case closed.

DA: *A bite mark matching her teeth, your DNA under her nails caught with a smoking gun. an affair, a web of lies victim's DNA on you will be lucky not to get the death sentence.*

Will: *But I didn't.*

DA: *Save it for the jury!*

The next morning back at the house Malix has bags packed, walks out to the porch and picks up the rosebush she has in a planter, it speaks to her.

The Voice: *You did it Malix, you gave them what they deserve. How does it feel?*

Malix: Empowering.

Chapter 5:
Learn to fly

Justin on the rooftop of his apartment building with Nadia. Trying to unlock his new powers.

Justin: *So I learned I can use power from the sun. I wonder what other earth energy I can harness*

Nadia*: wind can power flight*

Justin: *That would be awesome!!*

Nadia*: remember, these powers aren't for you to be awesome they are so you can protect the Earth from Cacodemonic while the supreme deity is away*

Justin*: got it… But still awesome. Here I go…. absorb the power of the wind.*

Justin closes his eyes and stands arms wide open as the wind blows leaves around him. His limp mohawk sways in the breeze. Justin gets lifted, and with a little more practice is now mastering the ability to fly

During his flight he sees below a group of protesters of the anti-homeless movement, the group is holding up signs, circling an alley, where the homeless are living. A homeless man speaks out to the rowdy crowd," leave us alone, we are out of sight in these back alleys, not causing any harm".

One of the protesters is videotaping the encounter to edit and try to get more anti-homeless followers Justin knew exactly what he was attempting ... being an empath with super powers and all.

One of the protesters knocks over boxes, which is someone's home. This starts a shove back-and-forth angry exchanges and a physical altercation one homeless man pulls a knife.

Justin flies down behind the crowd and walks his way up to the front where there's a fight, he sees the man videotaping and takes his phone.

Justin: *exploiting the situation to sway the mind of others that all homeless will be fighting in the streets, actions of one person does not define a whole community*

The man that had the camera lashes out at Justin, " this is our community we belong here, they belong in the sewers with the rats, not threatening our rights to protect our streets".

Justin*: controlling the streets, you mean, not "protecting"*

Justin smashes the guy's phone with his hand, then goes to the fight to break it up . He grabs the wrist of the homeless man who is holding a small knife. Justin feels his fear. He has no intent of using the knife, the man drops the knife, Justin stands between the protesters and some of the homeless. One of the protesters speaks up, "see they are dangerous, carrying knives!" Justin addresses the crowd," he was afraid and felt threatened. You came here, where they sleep, and started to knock down their shelters. ``

Justin reaches out to the protester, "Take my hand". The protest rolls his eyes," you Gotta be kidding me with this homeless love hippie bullshit"

Justin levitates... the crowd is shocked. The protester takes Justin 's hand. Justin takes his other hand to the homeless man. With each man holding one of Justin's hands, he works his empath powers. In this moment he can transfer emotions from both men. They come to realize there is no need to be enemies, the crowd disperse. The protester releases Justin's hand, " what did you just do?" Justin tells both men, " you were just able to feel each other's emotions, not clouded by judgment or self-righteousness. Not as men of different circumstances, but as spirits. Once all the superficial is gone and you see into someone's feelings..you understand we are ALL hurt the same." The two men shake each other's hand. Justin flys off to the top of a building stand with Nadia.

Nadia: *That was a wonderful use of your gifts, Internal, but that was a simple mortal squabble. When you encounter, the veins of Cacodemonic words will not save the day.*

Justin: *Creed was one of the three veins. When will I find the rest?*

Nadia: *in time they will find you*

The following day at the club, Justin's band setting up for their show. Bandmates setting up drums ask the guitar and bass player," we're on in five minutes. Where is Justin ?" The bass player responds, " I've text and called no answer".

Justin runs in wearing his work clothes janitors jumpsuit his mohawk limp

Justin: *I'm here... I gotta get ready. Got stuck at work.*

The drummer calls out to Justin," there's no time to change your clothes, we're on!" Justin goes into the dressing room throws hair gel in the stands up his mohawk A man announces the band to the crowd:

" Now everyone's favorite local, weird emo band, The Freaks!"

Justin turns to his band

Justin: *OK no need to change clothes I'll make it work guys let's open with some Rush*

The band goes on playing. Justin comes out onto the stage, playing a guitar on a mop they play Rush's Workingman. The audience loves it!

In the far back of the club a new fan is watching, standing in the corner it's... Malix. Later that night, outside the club after the show, Justin comes out the back door with his bandmates.

The band's guitar player congratulates his band mates," We rocked it, great job everyone! And Justin no more last-minute show up s, we need time to warm up"

Justin: *I'm sorry guys I got stuck working over...... you know they call me the working man*

They all laugh and say their goodbyes as they depart from the club, Justin stays a bit longer to talk to Tony the bouncer who is standing by the door.

Tony: *it's nice to see you in a better place Justin there's something different about you in a good way*

Justin: *thanks, Tony I've been not drinking away my feelings*

Tony: *That's good. Hey, you know your friend, the woman you were trying to help out?*

Justin: Roxanne?

Tony: yeah, I saw her working' the streets again

Justin: shit! When?

Tony: *Tonight, first time I've seen her out there since you tried to get her that job.*

Justin: *thanks Tony I'm going to find her*

Justin walks the city streets and then he finds Roxanne, a beautiful African American woman with long braids. She sees Justin & looks upset.

Roxanne: *Justin.. haven't seen you in a while... I'm just out for a walk.*

Justin: Roxanne, how long have we known each other?

Roxanne: Almost all our lives.

Justin: Right, and I know you...something's up.What happened to the job I helped you get?

Roxanne: I still have the job, but it's been a tough month. My nanna's Medicare is no longer covering the increase in her meds, that's where my paychecks went. Now I'm short on rent. Don't judge me.

Justin: I'm not judging you, believe me. This is dangerous work, and you are more than just a body and tricks. You're smart, funny and caring.

Roxanne: Justin, you think I want to be out here? I don't, but if I need to turn tricks to make rent this month then, so be it I am strong I won't be in danger.

Justin: I know you're strong... Did I mention stubborn, AF?

They share a laugh

Roxanne: you seem different

Justin: how?

Roxanne: sober

Justin: *I've cut back just a social drinker now, and you know, looking at life a little more positive attitude*

Roxanne: I wish I could, but life has a way of kicking me down. Existence starts to feel pointless. Every time something goes right, 5 other things go wrong.

Justin: I know, I get it... I've lived it. Don't give up, you need to believe.

Roxanne: Believe what...life gets better?

Justin: It can get better...existence is not pointless. Believe in something bigger than us. A car pulls up stops a bit ahead of them...a red sedan. Justin and Roxanne exchange looks.

Roxanne: we'll catch up soon

She walks towards the car. Justin walks away, Justin , thinking to himself.

"might go for one of those social drinks right about now"

Chapter 6: Bellicose

It's the year 2000, inside a small diner a nerdy man wearing large glasses, sits at a booth, and a waitress appears. The man Fred calls out for her, "Sherry "The waitress, Sherry turns to him, shocked to see him.

Sherry: *Fred what are you doing here? Where's Little Bell?*

Fred: *my niece came over to watch him. I needed a break that baby... our baby was screaming and crying nonstop since you came to work.*

Sherry: *You can't just show up at my job, Fred and he's probably got gas & newsflash babies cry.*

Meanwhile at their home, the niece and their baby has fiery red hair. The baby is screaming, nothing the niece does soothes his cries.

This was no ordinary baby. This baby, that was destined to find a vein of cacodemonic. This will not choose his path. It will, however, influence his soul, and tempt him to give into urges he was born with urges instilled in him, greater than what is born into your typical mortal child.

Flash forward 2006

Six year old Bellicose at the playground. His mom who has curly red hair and glasses is talking to another mom. Bellicose is ripping the heads off Barbie dolls his mom tells him to stop, but he throws a fit and kicks his mom. She is embarrassed. The other mom leaves and takes her daughter. Sherry calls out to her son.

Sherry: *let's go*

Bellicose: *NO!*

His mom gives up. The boy runs up to a place where the playground is empty, other than some workers landscaping in the far corner. Another mom walks up with her son. The boy goes to the slide. This new Mom starts a conversation with Little Bell's mom, " I wish I had their energy".

Sherry: *yeah, me too (she is nervous her son will act out again) my son is very energetic and unapologetic. I'm sorry I didn't mean to unload on you.*

Playground mom: *oh, no, dear don't be sorry*

Sherry: *I just fear he's different*

Playground mom: *maybe have him checked for a sensory disorder that could explain the behavior you're describing*

Little Bell's mom looks as if a lightbulb went off. Finally, a reason her son is so bad, she thinks to herself "sensory disorder". Little Bell starts approaching the other child.

Sherry: *Little Bell play nice!*

Playground mom: *Bell that's original name for a boy I like it*

Sherry: *it's short for Bellicose*

Playground mom: *very original*

The moms continue a nice conversation but Bellicose goes over to where the landscapers were. They went on break and left their equipment there, Bellicose picks up a shuffle.

Sherry: *no, Little Bell put that back, that's not a toy!*

Little Bell runs with the shovel

Playground mom: *it's just a shovel. Maybe he wants to help dig*

Little Bell goes up to the other little boy playing... he raises the shovel over his head

Little Bell's mom is running towards them. She shouts stop Little Bell, he hits the boy over the head with a shovel. The boy falls to the ground, crying.

Bellicose laughs, smiles, and laughs more. The other moms scoops up her son.

Sherry: *oh my God I'm so sorry*

Playground mom: *he gave him a concussion*

Later that day, Little Bell's parents (whose names are Fred and Sherry) are discussing the events of the day arguing.

Sherry: *it's not his fault, I think he has a sensory disorder*

Fred: *not his fault that kid went to the hospital Sherry he could be seriously injured. His parents could sue us.!*

Sherry: *I'm trying, Fred!*

(she starts to cry... Fred holds her)

Flash forward 2011 Little Bell is now 11 years old. Sherry is on the phone Little Bell is playing in the backyard

Sherry; *(on phone) yes mom I know but Bellicose is 11 and Sarah's girls are only eight.. he didn't mean to break it accidents do happen. You know he lost his temper when they started calling him a freak.*

(she pauses, she's listening to her mom rant on the other line) no I'm not saying it's an excuse to pull their hair, but they were purposely trying to trigger him. Everyone tries to make my son out as a problem child and I will take his side. (pauses again yelling coming out of the phone. Sherry yells back)... he has a sensory disorder!!!

hangs up the phone

Fred walks in from a long day at work

Sherry: *Fred you're home early*

Fred: *Only 30 minutes glad to be done. What a day. How about you? How was your day? He looks into the other room and sees Bellicose, playing with a hamster*

Fred: *You got a hamster and you didn't bother running past me?*

Sherry: *It's for him to learn empathy. I read about it online I I told you about the study.*

Fred: *you told me about a study you read you didn't ask to get a hamster and that's not how empathy works. You don't learn it you're born with it*

Sherry walks away

Fred: *(under his breath) and our son wasn't born with it*

Bellicose is in his room playing with the hamster with an evil look on his face. The hamster looks scared and tries to run away and hide Bellicose snatches him up

Later at dinner.

Sherry: *Little Bell, come eat*

All three sit at the table and eat dinner... parents make small talk

Fred: *Little Bell, what did you name your pet?*

Little Bell: *Jack like jack in a box*

Sherry: *that's clever, Little Bell*

Fred: *well, I would like to meet Jack after dinner*

Sherry: *oh, yes, that sounds like a great after dinner activity... meet and greet with Jack the hamster.*

After dinner, they walk to Little Belll's room

Lil Bell: *me and Jack had so much fun playing. Wait till you see him dad.*

Little Bill opens the door with a big evil grin

Sherry: *oh, my...*

Fred screams. They both cover their mouths in horror

In the backyard funeral for Jack the hamster

Sherry: *I don't understand how that could happen*

Fred is digging a hole

Little Bell: *it was an accident we were playing surgeon*

Fred: *That's no accident you Little...*

Fred *throws down the shovel*

Fred: *you know what you... dig the grave, Bellicose*

Fred *leaves, mother chases after him. Bellicose digs in the ground with a shovel. He finds a glowing orange light in the cracks of the soil. He puts the tip of the shovel into the light.*

Orange glow goes up the shovel into Bellicose's body, his eyes turn orange, he hears voices

Images in his brain... him pulling his cousins hair he grips to shovel and remembers hitting the boy with the shovel

Voice: *Embrace the violence...grow my iniquitous child. In a few years Cacodemonic will make you an offer ...grow strong boy...feed your need*

Now an image of Bellicoses picking up the hamster.

orange, light, dark and soul - fade out

Flash forward present day

Now an adult, Bellicose, sitting at the table, his mother, serving him dinner, adult Bellicose same fiery red hair, big built, like juggernaut Bellicose slams down his milk and wipes, his face and burps

Bellicose: *Done*

Sherry: *How about some dessert honey?*

Bellicose: *after shed work, mom*

Sherry: *oh, all the time you spend in that shed Little Bell you must be working on something pretty great!*

Bellicose: *(yelling) I'm not Little Bell I'm a man mom*

Sherry: *yes, yes sorry dear*

Bellicose takes off to the shed. Phone rings, Sherry answers it.

Sherry: *(on phone) Hi mom just cleaning up after dinner Little Bell... I mean Bellicose went out to his shed. (she pauses) It's not weird mom ever since Fred left us years ago the shed is where Bellicose goes to focus and control his anger (pause) Think what you want mom but ever since he had his own space in that shed his fits are less and less. (pause) No, I don't go in there cause.... he's a grown man and I respect his space.*

(sherry rolls her eyes)

Bellicose retired to his shed... of doom! The shed has many locks, inside is large, with steps that lead to an underground bunker. First part of the shed pans out tools... a shovel and rake, seems normal further...down scalpels and other surgical tools down the steps to the bunker, another set of locks. Behind the door is Bellicose sitting at a desk carving something. Around him jars of... eyeballs teeth, tongues

(Bellicose speaking to himself)

Bellicose: *I hurt them... I kill them Master Cacodemonic lets me. He gets their souls I get the blood! (he turns and we can see what he was carving. It's a human hand and he's taking the fingernails off. He places it down) Out of parts, time to hunt again*

Meanwhile, in the house, Sherry, still on the phone with her mother

Sherry: *It's a new recipe, Mom. you'll like it. (outside the kitchen window. She sees the car pull out of the garage) now sees mom Little Bell doesn't spend all his time in the shed. He just went out for a drive.*

Bellicose is out driving that night and he stops the car and rolls down the passenger side window. He holds up a $100 bill.

Bellicose: *get in*

Car door opens and a woman gets inside it… Roxanne!!!!!

Before she knows it Roxanne finds herself inside Bellicose's shed, gagged and tied up. She sees the jars of body parts.

Bellicose: *Are you scared? They bargain when they're scared... ha ha ha in the end I need something I can't cut off from you... something you must give me; you know what it is. They give me their souls, they give me their souls and I give them to the Master. It's easy because they can't see their soul so they don't think it's real. I tell them I'll stop hurting them. I'll let them go. but I don't! What do you want for your soul?*

He takes off her gag.

Roxanne: *you just told me you don't hold up your end of the deal*

Bellicose: *cause you already think you don't have a soul. you know, since you're a whore and all.*

Roxanne: *I don't know you, why would I give you anything?*

Bellicose: *you were going to give me your body for money, so why not give me your soul for a little mercy.... maybe some food. Want some food? My mom made dessert*

At this point, Roxanne knows he would have to leave to fetch the dessert.

'Tell him what he wants to hear, play into his game', She thinks to herself.

Roxanne: *you're right, no soul, so why not trade it for dessert*

Bellicose: *Good dessert!*

He puts the gag back on her mouth. Bellicose leaves to fetch dessert. Roxanne tries desperately to free herself. She sees a scalpel. she wiggles towards it. She frees one hand. She grabs the scalpel and is trying to cut the rest of the zip ties that bind her. She tries to escape the underground bunker but there's too many locks she's unable to.

Roxanne: *(to herself.) I am not giving up. There's gotta be a way out of here. I am getting out of here. I believe that! (she thinks of Justin's face the last time she saw him) I still believe Justin I still believe!*

Meanwhile across the city Justin is in bed, tossing and turning having a vivid nightmare, he hears Roxanne. He sees the shed. He awakens.

Justin: *Roxanne!!*

He quickly gets dressed and flies out the window, thinking to himself

"That was no dream, it was a vision. Roxanne is in danger. I can feel it. My heightened senses will lead me to her."

Meanwhile, inside Bellicose's mothers house, Bellicose walks in retrieving the cupcakes his mom made

Sherry: *Bellicose, is that you?*

His mom calls from the other room

Sherry: *Are you ready for dessert dear? How was your...*

Bellicose: (interrupting his mother) mom, you ask too many questions

His mom enters the room, sees him with a large plate of cupcakes and two glasses of milk

Sherry: *Do you want some help with that? Do you have a friend there?*

Bellicose: *yes, we're playing surgeon*

Sherry: *oh, that's great I want to come meet them*

Bellicose: *no, you stay here it's my shed you stay out I mean it mom*

Bellicose leaves taking the cupcakes to the shed. He starts to unlock the door to the underground bunker on the other side of the door. Roxanne waits, holding a scalpel ready to fight. Bellicose enters his hands full with dessert and cups of milk.

Bellicose: *chocolate cupcakes for my chocolate girl!*

Roxanne jumps on his back and stabs him in the shoulder. He swings Roxanne off his back. She falls, he picks her up and throws her across the room.

Bellicose: *(covering his wounded shoulder) you hurt me, you tricked me*

He swings at her. She's fast and avoids his swing. Bellicose looks down at the spilt milk and plate.

Bellicose: *you made me drop the cupcakes!*

He grabs her and takes a scalpel and cuts off her pinky finger. She screams loudly.

Bellicose: *stop it! shut up my mom will hear you*

He gags her.. the door starts to open, Bellicose thinking it is his mom goes to shut the door

Bellicose: *no mom, I said stay out!*

The door gets kicked down, Bellicose is shocked and so is Roxanne. The doors kicked down by Justin the Internal!

Justin, fueled by emotions.. Roxanne's fear and pain burst into the room, punches bellicose so hard he knocks a tooth out. He slams his fist into Bellicose over and over Bellicose grabs the Internal by the neck and pushes him up against the wall. Roxanne, scared, runs out to find help. The Internal cannot get out of Bellicose's hold. He takes his hand and pushes on Bellicose's temples. This is working to weaken bellicose, but it's also weakening Justin 's emotions as he's absorbing so much from Bellicose's rage, hate, violence! Bellicose drops to his knees,The Internal pushes his head so tight, his eyes bleed

Justin: *I should kill you, you monster what you did to her... to all these people?*

The Internal pushes Bellicose out of the bunker into the shed inside The Internal picks up a blade and the jar of eyeballs.

Justin: *Eye for an eye*

He stabs Bellicose in the eye, he sees Roxanne's pinky finger on the floor, fresh with blood, her distinct nail polish on it.

Justin: *you took her (He then cuts off, Bellicose's finger) I should take your life the world be better off*

Suddenly sirens are heard. ..red and blue lights flashing. The Internal grabs the hanging tie wraps. He wraps up Bellicose and picks up Roxanne's finger. Roxanne is standing outside the shed waving over the cops. The Internal gives Roxanne her severed finger.

Justin: *get this on ice*

He flies off. Sherry is outside as the police take her son into custody

Sherry: *no wait he didn't do anything*

Cop: *ma'm he's a serial*

Sherry: *It's not his fault..... he has a sensory disorder!*

Chapter 7:
Not Without Flaws

Justin is drinking in his place alone feeling disgusted with Bellicose, his feelings, his reaction. Nadia appears

Nadia: *The Internal struggles*

Justin*: That was more than I expected the evil I encountered... that monster! Roxanne, a good woman, nearly lost her life and I lost control. I absorbed too much of Bellicose and I can still feel his sick thoughts inside of me ...or are they my sick thoughts? Roxann, a person I know and care for deeply. When I saw her hurt, I lost control. I wanted to kill him, not stop him, but end him all together. My goodness dimmed and my rage shined through. I'm supposed to stop evil, not become it!*

Nadia *you're not to be without flaws you are only mortal. Anger is one of the many emotions all mortals feel this does not overshadow you're good intentions*

Justin: *But I never felt... That... So intense before.*

Nadia: *because you never absorb pure evil before the near fact that you can acknowledge those feelings, and that they're intensity fears you shows that the rage is not your intention, it was transferred from Bellicose*

Justin: *And when do I stop that... When do I feel completely me again?*

Nadia: *it shall pass, do not let this define you. learn from it and move on*

Justin: *spoken like a true nonhuman*

He takes another drink

Nadia: *Perhaps you should get off your pity horse and check on the life you just saved*

Justin: *Perhaps ... (he pauses and thinks before he chooses his next words) You are right He puts the bottle down realizing he's sulking, and that there is more to him than what just happened.*

Later that day, Justin walks into Roxanne's hospital room and brings her flowers (a poor man's bouquet)

Roxanne: *Hello hero*

He hands her the flowers.

Justin: *hero?*

Roxanne: *Am I not to know you're The Internal? Cause if so, Dude, that mohawk is a dead giveaway.*

Justin: *it's a lot to explain & I will at some point(he sees her wrapped up finger) I see they were able to reattach your finger*

Roxanne: *yes, and I'm actually getting out of here now. Wanna walk a girl home?*

Justin smiles. Roxanne signs papers and leaves the hospital. She and Justin have a nice walk. Roxanne shares details of her encounter with Bellicose.

Roxanne: *How did you find me?*

Justin: *I'm not sure I had a dream I saw you, you needed me. The rest of it felt like built-in GPS*

Roxanne: *I did need you. I'm so thankful Justin, he was going to kill me and take my soul*

Justin: *soul?*

Roxanne: *yes, he doesn't just kill he takes 's souls*

Justin: *What did he say?*

Roxanne: *He said he gives them to his master. It's real. I saw the people's souls.*

Justin: *I believe you and you're alive and for that I am thankful*

They arrive to Roxanne's apartment outside her door they say their goodbyes

Roxanne: *and Justin , thank you for the flowers*

Chapter 8:
My Human Life

Justin and Nadia are in the apartment.

Nadia: *you appear in a much better state of mind, Internal have you shedded off the lasting effects of absorbing Bellicose?*

Justin: *I can still feel a bit of Bellicose's presence, but being around someone who's Aurora is warm and welcoming, overpowers that*

Nadia: *Roxanne, I take it?*

Justin: *YES and I found out something from her, something Bellicose did, and I need to understand why... he collected souls of his victims for his master.... has to be Cacodemonic. I think he is planning to emerge for the Earth's core & use the captured souls to take over.*

Nadia: *That is most troubling indeed. I can travel far enough into the multiverse to try to get a message through to the supreme deity. This needs to be brought to his attention.*

Justin: *OK and what do I do while you're gone?*

Nadia: *do not look for Cacodemonic's third vein in my absence. Rest and regroup Internal. Mortals need more rest than spirit guide's I shall return*

Nadia takes off. Justin sits down, plays guitar, reads a book, looks at a photo on his refrigerator of Roxanne.

Justin thinking to himself:

Justin: *OK so surprise but I haven't ever been in a relationship. I've seen inside hundreds of people's relationships. You know the whole empath that absorbs people's energy I've absorbed, so many emotions, relationships, full of ups and downs. If it's not up and down then it's boredom or just settling which many do. I hear* *they're hidden emotions they're yearning for deep connection and romance. I'm not saying those types of relationships are bad, but they do lie to themselves at least from time to time. Now the feeling you get when there's a new love when someone makes you smile all day no matter what you're doing and they are in your thoughts all day all night even when you dream. That is new love.*

It puts a skip in your step and makes you feel like you are radiating sunshine. Seeing that person makes you excited, but nervous… alive! Their scent, their voice, their essence brings you utter joy most people only get that feeling once maybe twice in their lives. the. For me I get the feeling that over and over. So fresh, so blissful I loved feeling their love but after 30 times or so I don't wanna feel up again... like I said ups and downs, there's always. Some people work through it and that leads to that settled safe feeling, some people don't. Some people feel crazy in their downs, the amount of emotions. heartbreak brings a lot… too much. It can cloud their rational thoughts and shatter their dreams, feeling that part over and over knowing the outcome, the red flags, the lies and the things that just aren't meant to be. That's why I don't do relationships. I think of all that, reflecting is inspiring me to write a song, the best part of being an intense empath. we can turn raw emotion into music, beautiful, powerful, goosebumps giving music!

Justin grabs a pen paper and his guitar

A few days pass as Justin lives his normal life. Coming and going to work, band practice, him eating cereal, thinking to himself." When will Nadia return". He gets dressed for work in his janitor clothes.

Thinking to himself," today I get to show the ropes to a new trainee."

He is at his job cleaning a football stadium. His new coworker is... Roxanne.

Roxanne: *thanks so much for getting me this job, Justin, a side cleaning gig will help me make ends meet while helping my grandma.*

Justin: *don't thank me yet you haven't seen the post-game mess*

They enter the stadium, the bleachers covered in trash. He hands her a bag and a broom.

Justin: *There is one bonus, though. (he shakes his large work keys) We get to use the private restrooms. They both laugh. Next scene is Justin walking Roxanne home after work.*

Justin thinking to himself" I'm glad Roxanne is working with me. I'm happy she's able to make more money and I'm happy to have a friend at work."

Outside of Roxanne's apartment.

Justin: *I have a show tomorrow, you should come.*

Roxanne: *I would but I have a date planned.*

Justin's face freezes, as this news is very devastating to his feelings for her.

Justin: *Oh, I didn't know you were seeing someone. Do I need to run a background check on him? (he has an uncomfortable laugh)*

Roxanne: That's not necessary. We met while I was in the hospital, he was my resident dr.

Justin: *Oh, wow, a Dr..that's great*

Roxanne smiles, Justin smiles back even though he feels sad for himself, he feels her happiness. After all, when you truly care for someone you want them to be happy, even if it's not with you.

Justin is walking home; a woman is walking behind him with a large paper bag of groceries blocking her view. She walks right into Justin, her groceries fall, he helps her pick them up. The woman is Malix. She's wearing a hat and gloves, casual clothes, her makeup is spot on and her shirt is of a local band called 'Rug Burn'.

Justin: *Nice shirt, you're a fan?*

Malix: *yes, I go to most of their local shows*

Justin: *No way, that's awesome. My band is opening for them tomorrow at the club.*

Malix: *Really, what's the name of your band?*

Justin: *the freaks we're kind a punk emo with a classic rock core*

Malix: *I've heard of them.*

They are bent down, picking up the spilled groceries. Justin picks up a big eggplant.

Justin: *that some of the biggest produce I've seen*

Malix: *well, a single woman needs to eat*

She smiles, seductively and takes the eggplant from his hands and places it into the bag Justin blushes

Justin: *sorry I ran into you and spilled your groceries*

Malix: *accidents happen no biggie. So you're in the Freaks what's your name in case I want an autograph or something ha ha*

Justin: *Justin and what's your name?*

Malix: *Malix*

Justin puts his hand out to shake her hands but her hands are full

Justin: *nice to meet you, my Malix*

Malix: *likewise, Justin thanks for helping me pick these up even if it was your fault they dropped. See you around.*

She walks away. Justin grins and walks away.

Chapter 9:
Long Cool Woman

Malix is thinking to herself after her encounter with Justin...' I found him the one I am to stop. I played it off pretty cool too... My staged coincidence?'

She's home now, puts the bag of food, takes her gloves and hats off thinking to herself...

'Gloves to avoid skin to skin contact, hat to cover up brain waves band shirt that would lead to conversation through music. She removes the produce and unbagged the giant eggplant a little innuendo and just like that... I'm in his mind and not the other way around. She smiles as she goes to her glowing rosebush now in her new apartment. It speaks.

The Voice: *You found him now you must stop him.*

The next day the club Justin's band is performing after the show Justin goes to the bar for water. He chugs it down. Malix is sitting next to where he is standing, but facing the other way. She is dressed to kill, strong, sexy punk rock. She turns around and is now face to face with Justin.

Malix: *thirsty?*

Justin: *Malix, hi didn't recognize you without the bag of groceries ha ha*

Malix: *good show*

Justin: *Thanks, glad you came. I mean cool that you made it.*

Malix: *let me buy you a drink for such a strong performance*

She walks across the bar to order drinks.

Justin is thinking to himself: ' OK well she's cool and beautiful... weird I can't get a read on her Aurora. I mean nice, not weird. I've wanted to quiet all the noise and emotions when I'm living my normal life besides reading off people is kind of like spying.'

Malix walks back with two drinks.

Justin to himself:' Maybe it's OK. Just enjoy a little normal. The internal's quest is kinda on hold till Nadia returns.'

Malix holds up her drink

Malix: *cheers to great show*

They toast and drink

They are talking about music, enjoying a drink

Justin: *well, it was nice chatting with you, but I should be going*

Malix: *What? We only had one drink?*

Justin: *I actually don't drink much any more*

Malix: *You don't need a drink to socialize.. bartender, one more for me and a water for my pal here*

 Justin: *you got me there*

Malix: *Now can we finish our conversation of the top five bands of all time?*

They sit and chat and laugh for another hour

Malix: *This has been so much fun Justin but I guess now I should be getting home Justin is looking at the time on his phone. They exit the club.*

Justin: *maybe I'll see you another show*

Malix: *yeah, maybe.... you're gonna walk me home, right?*

Justin: *I don't know where you*

Malix: *It's not far from here you wouldn't want a pretty girl walking the streets alone at this hour, would you?*

Justin: *no, definitely not*

Malix: *Besides, I heard there was a serial killer caught recently in the city. He locked up women in the shed or something.*

Justin: *mostly women, but men too*

Malix: *oh, you know the details huh? Spill it.*

Justin: *no, I just read about it that's all*

Malix: *hey, you're a bit of a mystery Justin Young*

Justin: *What me? nah*

They get to Mailx's apartment. Outside she invites him in for a drink.

Justin:*I shouldn't*

Malix: *You had one drink an hour and a half ago! come on one glass of wine.*

Malix makes a pouty face

Justin: *OK (smiles)*

They go into the apartment. Justin sits in a chair in the living room while Malix pours wine in the kitchen.

Justin thinking to himself:' Why did I agree to this? She's nice, but I don't know her. I don't date. This isn't a date, OK just chill.'

Malix is in the kitchen and she looks at her rose it glows.

The Voice: *Don't let me down, he's in your hooks, finish it!*

Malix thinking to herself: ' just keep him talking..lights out complete my task.'

She walks into the livingroom and hands Justin a glass of wine then sits on the couch

Malix: *so, Justin, how long ago did you start your band??*

Justin: *(sipping his wine) we started in high school just a few wanna be punk rock stars we've come a long way from playing in our parents basements*

Malix: *How did you guys come up with your band name?*

Justin: *Well, we were a group of Misfit, but that band name was already taken. Ha ha so we called ourselves what we felt like... the freaks. Now enough questions about me, I'm not self-absorbed, I don't need to talk all about me.. as I am doing right now. You, Malix, I can't get a read on...tell me about you.*

She's thinking to herself-' what kind of reverse psychology is this shit he barely touched that drink'

Malix: *me, I recently moved to the city from the suburbs*

Justin: *OK now I'm learning. what made you decide to move?*

She takes a large drink

Malix: *oh, I moved because of a bad break up.I wanted, I needed a fresh start*

Justin: *Interesting I didn't get a hurt vibe from you. You come across so strong and cool*

Malix: *Well, dear Justin, I never said I was hurt and I am strong and cool. ha ha I finished my drink, let me top off yours*

She grabs Justin 's, half full glass of wine and her empty glass and walks into the kitchen. The rose bush is glowing.

The Voice: *Do you like being a fool? I thought I opened your eyes to the real world. Guess all it takes to pull the wool over your eyes is attention from a man. pathetic*

Malix who went from a smile when she entered the kitchen is now furious

Malix: *I am no fool. I am fooling him!*

Voice: *finish the job, prove you're as strong as you claim you are*

She puts more drugs in the Justin 's drink and returns to the living room

Justin: *thank you, and you are most certainly strong & Cool. Moving out of town is a big step that must've been a seriously bad break up. I'm sorry, I don't mean to pry, I was just curious about you.*

Malix: *that's OK ask away*

Justin: *you picked a good city to move to, great local bands places to go, parking sucks but that's why I mostly walk*

Malix: *So tell me Justin have you ever been in a seriously bad break up?*

Justin: *well, no, cause I never had a serious relationship*

Malix: *never?*

Justin: *nope, I kinda coward away from them. I feel like... Like I've seen too much heartache that overrides the good feelings that comes with love*

Malix: *that's your problem, right there you believe in love*

Justin: *And you don't?*

Malix: *There's no such thing as love, just lus. People don't fall in love with a person for who they are, they fall in love with the idea of what kind of life they can have with that person. What that person has that benefits their lives... It can be they like having a good looking partner, it boosts their own self-confidence, or they can be a weak person, wanting to leach onto someone strong, live through them. They might want money or their lifestyle, but sure enough it has nothing to do with the actual person. Love is a fantasy, it's not real it's exploiting feelings for one's own idea of love.*

Justin: *Wow, that's deep and you make a lot of great points. It can be like that but, as real as it may seem, I still believe there is real love*

Malix: *then, maybe you're a fool*

Justin squints his eyes.His vision goes blurred ,his eyes feel like led. He thinks to himself-' this isn't right what's happening'. He lays on the floor conscious but unable to move, struggling to stay awake.

Malix: *sorry, Justin I have a task, and you have a foolish heart*

Justin: *(barely able to speak) what... Task?*

Malix: *I was like you once.. innocent, naïve, kind and you know where that got me? Fucked over, used a laughingstock at my job, I was the fool. Then my eyes were opened by a carrier for Cacodemonic.*

Justin's eyes widen as he lays in a puddle of his own drool

Malix: *Once I accepted his blood oath, everything was clear he helped me get revenge. He helped me evolve. With his help,I took my power back. All he asked in return is the souls of people, trash like the users in my life. The soul, he demands, the cherry on top of his soul Sunday.... Well that's you, Justin*

She turns towards Justin, he is helpless. He sees her smile. He sees her now for what she is not who she pretended to be. He thinks to himself' get up', but he can't. He can barely keep his eyes open.

Malix: *takes her long gloves off, revealing razor-like fingernails. She runs one up his thigh, cutting his skin. He bleeds. She grabs his head.*

Malix: *now it's time to serve my master, and receive all the rewards that come with it*

She pulls out a razor nail to cut his throat. Just then a force breaks through the window, knocking her to the wall. It's Nadia.

Nadia: *the internal come with me*

Wind like hands lift up, Justin. Thanks to Nadia he escapes this near death situation. Nadia returns Justin to his apartment, letting him rest off the drugs that were in the wine.

Nadia, thinking to herself: 'in the escape Internal, you found the third vein of cacodemonic, false appearance lured you in. Now that all three veins have failed to take you. I fear we will soon see the creator of all darkness, the vile, nefarious cacodemonic

Chapter 10: The Awakening

Justin awakes to sirens outside his window. He looks outside and there's chaos! Fires out in the street, people vandalizing buildings, and vehicles.

Nadia: _The sirens are echoing' closer. The darkness is coming out. Most mortals are choosing evil over good. We are losing the battle, virtue is disappearing. It is their free will to choose, but cacodemonic has fed into their doubt through emotions fueled with just anger there. Hope is gone._

Justin: _It's my mission to give them hope. Were you able to contact the Supreme Deity?_

Nadia: _no Internal, he was several light years away from me. I returned to Earth as soon as I felt your body weaken. I did send out a message to tell the Supreme Deity that we learned of Cacodemonic, capturing souls of mortals. As of right now the world out there is losing all nobility, show them Internal show them... all is not lost._

Justin lights up, transforming into his superhero alter ego, powering up, THE INTERNAL! He flies out the window. Good people the world look out their windows, while the wicked destroy the city. Their eyes widen, jaws drop, as they see the bright white light of the internal as he flies down to the ground. A little girl on the balcony above the chaos with her mom the girl says:" mom who is that?"

mom replies:" that's who's going to save us"

Several disgruntled people stop and lay down their weapons shocked at what they see, a man flying. Justin lands down and tries to reason with the irate herd.

Justin: *people please stop this rage, this destruction. I know you feel anger, but do not lose connection to your other feelings, hope, happiness, love, those feelings maybe be blurred right now. Those feelings are buried right now, as he grows and tries to take over you, but you are not gone! You are not overtaken, you've just been misguided. I ask you, lay down your arms and surrender to the good that is still in you, it's there you just have to find it.*

Several people in the mob drop their weapons. One person says:' "he is right we lost our way"

Other people in the mob don't come to realize that. They begin to mock the eternal. One man in the mob exclaims, "I have no buried goodness, I have a buried wife and son! They were killed in a car accident. You expect me to be full of love and happiness when life has brought me nothing but hurt?" A woman in the mob chimes in, "yes, all this goodness is easy for the rich while we working class bust our ass to make them richer! We work, just to scrape by, no vacations, no time for leisure, we work, pay taxes and die, that's it!"

Justin: *I'm sorry... I'm sorry life is not perfect. It is a struggle. I know this, but we must not give up. We all have paths. It's up to us to decide which one to take.*

Just then an earthquake strikes, the ground cracks open. Demons pour out and begin to attack everyone. The mob screams and runs, but are captured and dragged into the cracks of the earth's core, the place inhabited by Cacodemonic.

A battle begins, The Internal is fighting demons with his powers. More demons emerge and overpower the internal. The good people that have been watching from the apartment windows start to throw items at the demons, an attempt to help The Internal. Several members of the mob that came to their senses also fight off the demons. The Internal flys and uses his powers to destroy many of the demons that were climbing up the buildings trying to get to the people inside. Another earthquake strikes, day becomes night. Breaking out the earth's crust is Cacodemonic! He throws down his roots of evil, that wrap up the people on the ground, their eyes turn white, he takes their souls and they now fight on his side.

Cacodemonic: *Justin Young, the powerful empath, the one chosen to show the world goodness & hope... you have failed.(He grabs the internal)It took me a millennium to persuade mortals to choose evil over good. I could not take away their free will, but I could convince them to give it to me. (as he speaks to the people of the mob now with eyes glowing white raise up and fight for him) This means I win this planet created by your supreme deity that he left is now mine to rule and these demons you fight are formed from the souls I have captured. The souls are now my army and will fight for me!*

He squeezes Justin, but Nadia swoops in like a breeze, freeing him from Cacodemonic's grip. Justin fights Cacodemonic, but the mob now white eyed and possessed attacks Justin. He gets beaten, bloodied, bruised. Cacodemonic slaps Nadia across the Earth. He picks up Justin .

Cacodemonic: *Now, for the ultimate soul, join me, I will give you power far beyond what you can even imagine. Rule beside me, no more feelings that plagued you. With me you will only feel power.*

Justin 's eyes swollen face bleeding, he looks up

Justin: *never, I'll never join you. You can hurt me. You can kill me, but you cannot take my free will The Supreme Deity gave it to me to us all and you cannot take it.*

Cacodemonic: *you fool, loyal to your creator, the supreme deity he created you then abandoned you. Here I am taking over his humans and he doesn't even care!*

Just then a mighty bolt of lightning strikes.... The Supreme Deity is flying down on a white steed

Supreme Deity: *I am not here to care.... (he points to Justin) He is!*

(The Supreme Deity lifts Justin up) I am the creator, he is the compassion!

Supreme Deity, and Justin are lifted into the clouds leading to a dimension far away from Earth. The Supreme deity, heals Justin, he gives Justin a drink from his gold goblet. Justin sits up, getting his strength back.

Justin: *we gotta get back and stop him*

Supreme Deity: *I will form another planet for you to live on. One that Cacodemonic can never find, never corrupt*

Justin: *what? The people of Earth are down, their suffering cacodemonic is ruling them.*

Supreme Deity: *they let him win they made their choices*

Justin: *no, not all of them did.. there is still good there... in everyone*

Supreme Deity: *they you ridiculed you*

Justin: *but now they're eyes are open*

Supreme Deity: *you are sure they are worth saving?*

Justin: *yes, they are and they need to know who you are*

Supreme Deity: *all right, then prepare for battle*

The Supreme Deity gathers his soldiers on white horses. They enter Earths, fighting the demons, lifting up humans in saving them. The supreme deity fights Cacodemonic, the internal is fighting along their side. The supreme deity slams his sector into Cacodemonic's chest. This causes an explosion of bright, white light, it destroys Cacodemonic. The demons start to shrink and get pulled back into the crack where they emerged. The supreme deity taps the ground with his scepter and the crack closes.

The Supreme Deity turns to Justin

Supreme Deity: *the Earth is safe from Cacodemonic , but there are more evil entities amongst us, amongst the universe. The fate of the humans is up to them. The fate of their planet is up to them... to care for it.*

Justin: *And me, I return to making music?*

Supreme Deity: *oh, no, you are more than a mortal musician Justin. You must use your gift to remind people of compassion and humidity. And fight against the forces that threaten this Justin what you can feel inside you and others is what makes you The Internal, don't take that for granted. Now I must depart there's work for me elsewhere, farewell Internal*

Justin watches the supreme deity fly away into space. Days after the event there is news showing clips of people who were in the area being interviewed. Justin watches it on TV with Roxanne and Nadia.

One news clip is of a woman she says: " it was crazy. There were rioters and demons.. the superhero man flew down and stopped them. Then there was an earthquake, and then total darkness."

A man being interviewed:" yeah, I saw the superhero said his name was Eternal like he's immortal something"

Another man:" there was a riot in the streets and an earthquake. The darkness was clouds. There's a logical reason for this: the so-called superhero was probably someone who wants to be some type of vigilante."

Another person's comments on the news clips: "There were supernatural forces. It was war, heaven and hell the Lord saved us."

News reporter: *there you go multiple witnesses with different versions of what happened in the city. After losing electricity, an earthquake and some kind of solar eclipse. I spoke to another young man earlier today that has his own opinion of the events.*

The reporter then interviews Justin.

Reporter: *After these hyper normal events what do you make of the arrival of this alleged superhero The Internal?*

Justin: *I think he came with a message.*

reporter: *and what would that message be?*

Justin: *BELIEVE*

The End